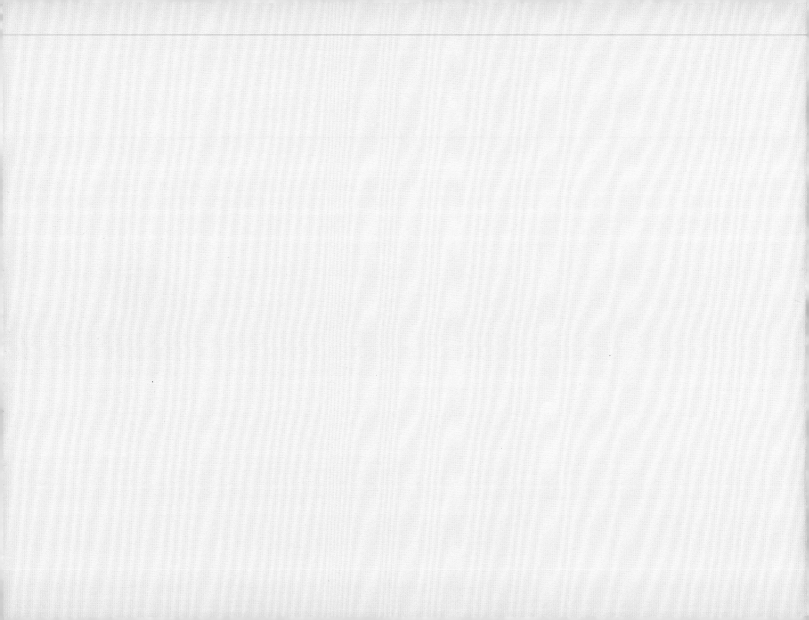

EDDIE SPAGHETTI

Rutu Modan

BASED ON THE WORK OF

ARYEH NAVON AND LEA GOLDBERG

FANTAGRAPHICS BOOKS

"EDDIE SPAGHETTI GETS DRY"

Oh, what a day! Bright, clear, and pretty,
Eddie decided to leave the city.

He walked on his way, taking time to explore,
When at once the skies opened — it started to pour!

Eddie ran home, but he started to fret.
Eddie Spaghetti was so very wet.

"How will I get dry?" Eddie heard himself whine.

Then he hung himself up, just like that, on the line.

Eddie Spaghetti woke up so early,
Grabbed his bucket and line and headed out to the sea.

He dipped his line into waves deep and blue,
In search of a fish, or perhaps quite a few.

He stood and he fished and he pulled out his line,
But it looked like he'd have to wait a long time.

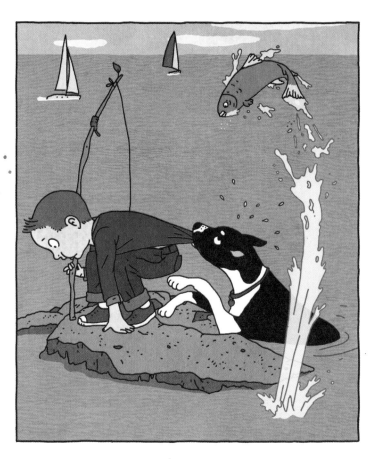

They say that it takes lots of patience to fish,
So Eddie just sat there, alone with his wish.

What's happened at sea? Is it as Eddie feared?
Had all of the fish swam away? Disappeared?

Eddie got up to go home, and he took
His bucket for fishing, his line, and his hook.

"Why did I wait for so long?" Eddie said.
He fished for a goldfish in his own house instead.

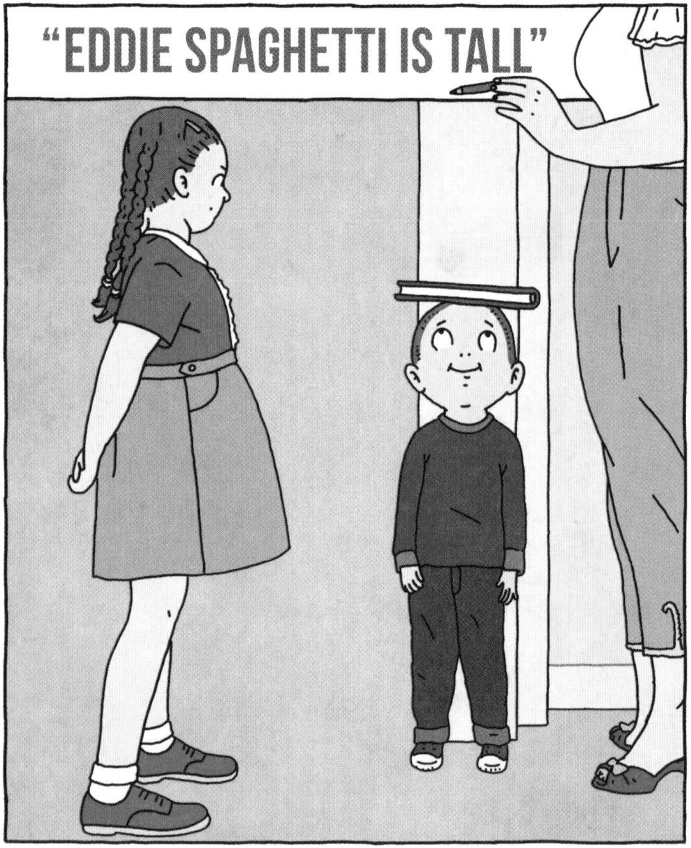
"EDDIE SPAGHETTI IS TALL"

Eddie Spaghetti is standing up tall.
Mom measures him — but he is not tall at all.

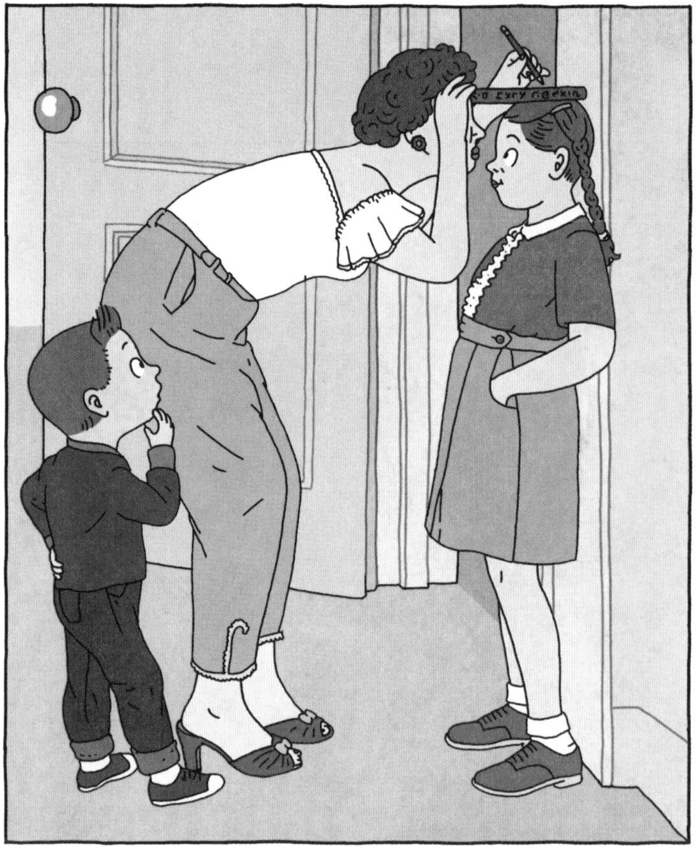

"This is not good," Eddie said with a snort.
"I do not like it that I am so short."

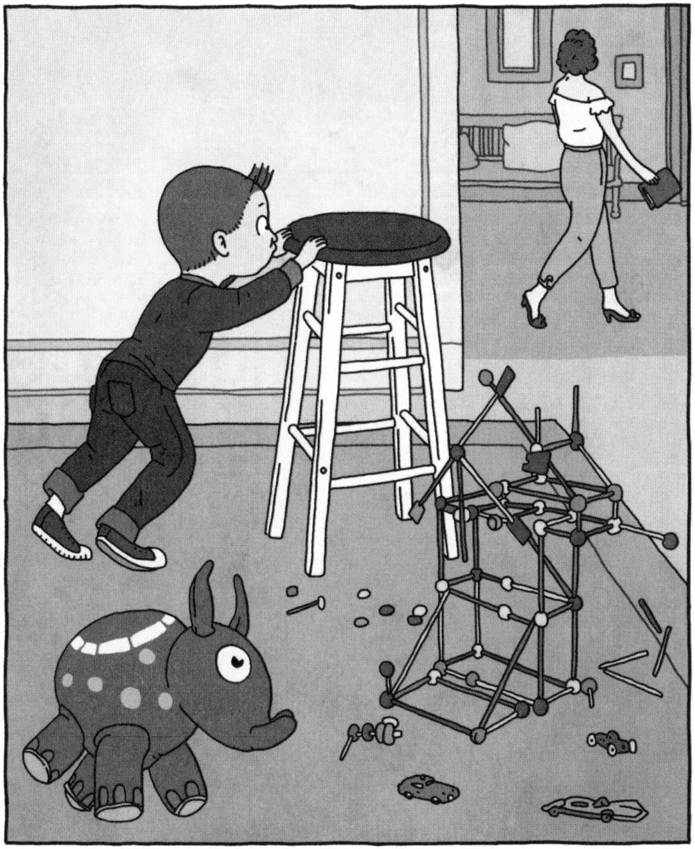

"I may be small, but I'm surely no fool."
He ran to his room and came back with a stool.

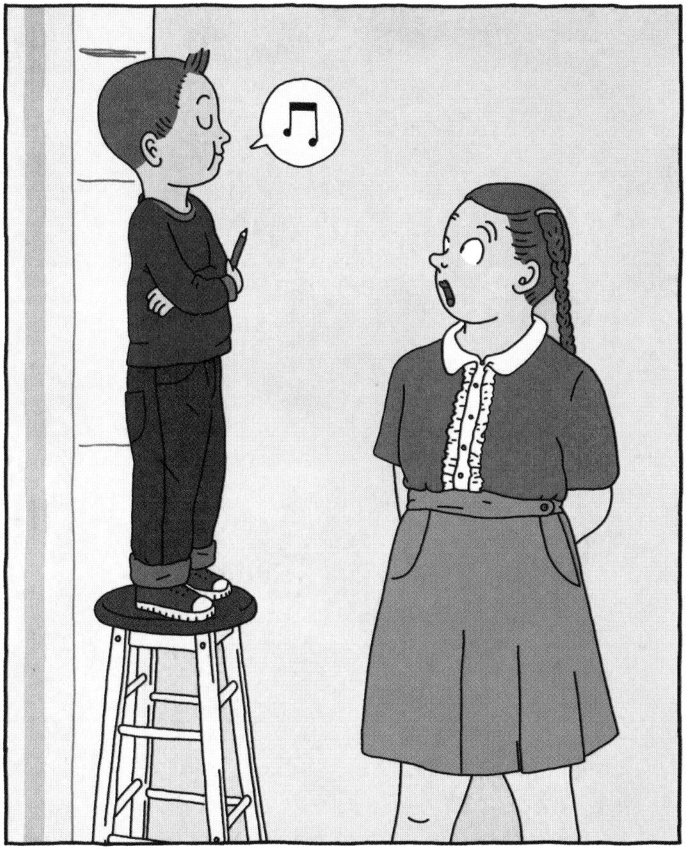

Eddie stood on the stool, enjoying the view.
"Look," he said proudly, "at how fast I grew!"

"EDDIE SPAGHETTI ON THE TRAIN"

As the train rushed through the green countryside,
Eddie sat calmly, enjoying the ride.

He ate a banana — it tasted quite good.
He wanted to throw out the peel, as he should.

But there was no trash bin, the windows were sealed —
Eddie had no place to toss out his peel.

And then, in a flash, he knew just what to do.
He pulled the emergency lever — it's true!

The train stood unmoving, the cops ran so fast,
The crowds disembarked. Eddie pushed his way past.

What happened here? Did something go awry?
The passengers elbowed their way to espy —

And Eddie Spaghetti completed his feat.
He threw out the peel and returned to his seat.

"EDDIE SPAGHETTI SETS OUT ON A TRIP"

A map and a hat, leather shoes with good grip —
Eddie Spaghetti sets out on a trip.

"Do I have all that I need for my quest?"
Eddie is hoping to make it out west.

The journey is long and his faithful dog jockeys.
Maybe he'll head on the map to the Rockies?

Spread out the map. Trample westward. Anon!
Eddie arrives at the sea before long.

Eddie Spaghetti does not like to sit.
His small body just doesn't quite fit.

Eddie knows just what to do.
He saws the table legs — one, and then two.

A problem now of a different sort.
Eddie finds the table too short!

So, quick quick, with no time to spare,
Eddie cuts the legs off his chair.

Oh no, Eddie, that will not do!
Now the chair is too short for you!

Once again, he gives it a go.
He cuts the table legs below.

Eddie, Eddie boy — oh no!
The table is again too low!

Without a table or a chair,
Look how well our Eddie fares.

Eddie stands on the curb on a wet, rainy morn.
The street is all muddy, Eddie's feeling forlorn.

A car rushes past and — splash! — like a flood,
Eddie Spaghetti is splattered in mud.

Covered in filth, from head to toe,
There is only one place that poor Eddie can go.

He runs to his house and jumps in the tub.
"I'll rinse in the water, I'll soak and I'll scrub."

Eddie sits in his clothes,
But he only gets wetter.

What would you say?
Are things really much better?

And what to do now?
The water's too high!

Eddie walks out
so he can get dry.

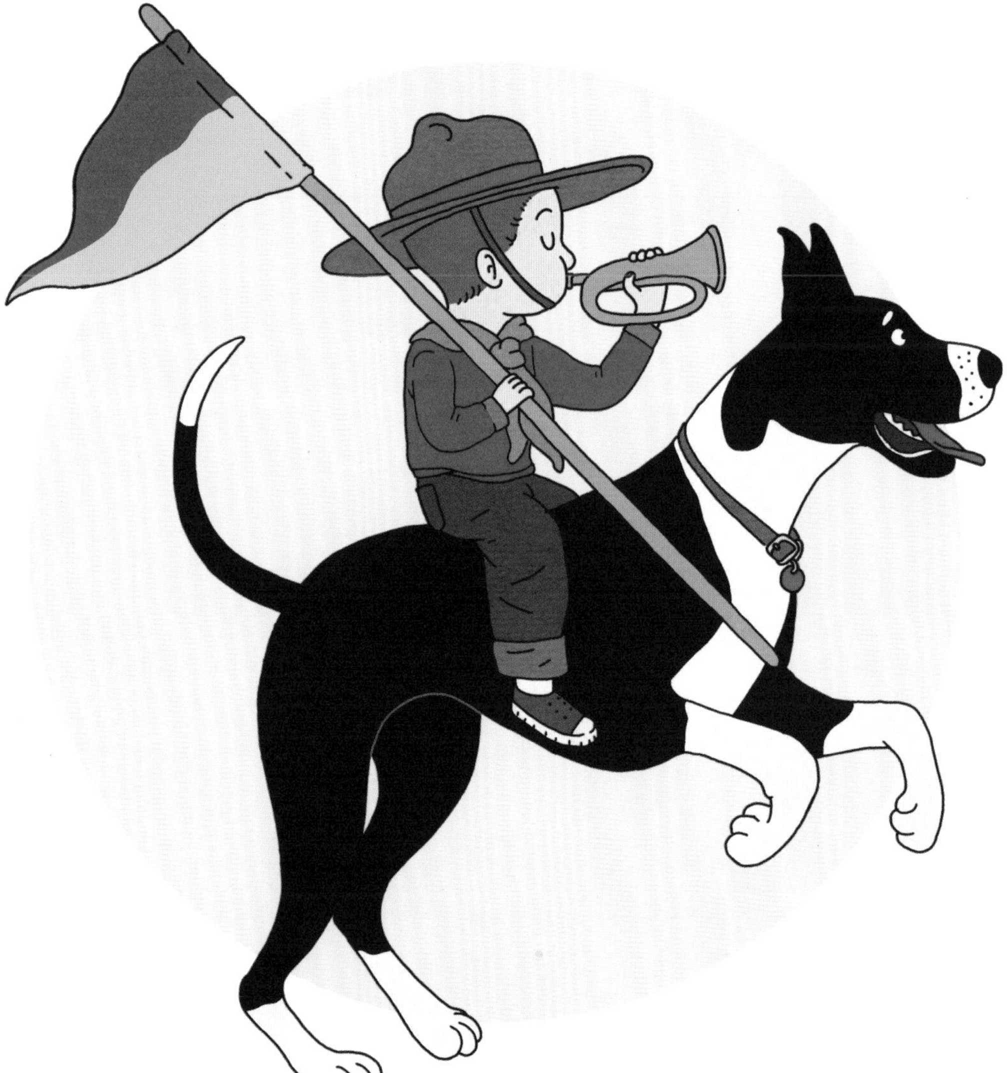

Eddie Spaghetti, one of the oldest and most popular comic characters in the Hebrew language, was the brainchild of the artist and cartoonist Aryeh Navon, a founding father of Israeli graphic arts. Eddie Spaghetti came into the world in the middle of the 1930s. Navon, who worked for the periodical *Davar La'Yeladim*, would think up a different plotline to illustrate each week.

Lea Goldberg, the celebrated Israeli poet, worked for the same weekly publication and composed rhyming narration for each comic strip. The collaboration between the poet and the artist was beloved by Israeli children: The many comic strips they created were published over the years, and with time other characters were added into the mix, no less hilarious and mischievous than Eddie Spaghetti.

As a tribute to the original creativity of Aryeh Navon and Lea Goldberg, and on the eightieth anniversary of Eddie Spaghetti, the graphic artist Rutu Modan has illustrated her version of some of these delightful tales.

Translator: Ilana Kurshan
Editor: Conrad Groth
Designer: Jacob Covey
Supervising Editor: Gary Groth
Associate Publisher: Eric Reynolds
Publisher: Gary Groth

Fantagraphics Books, Inc.
7563 Lake City Way NE
Seattle, WA 98115

www.fantagraphics.com
Facebook.com/Fantagraphics
@fantagraphics.com

ISBN: 978-1-68396-177-2
Library of Congress Control Number: 2018949541
First Fantagraphics Books edition: February 2019
Printed in Malaysia